Boobela
and Worm
Ride the
Waves

Also in this series ...

Boobela and Worm

Boobela and the Belching Giant

Boobela, Worm and Potion Power

Boobela and Worm, Ace Detectives

Boobela
and Worm
Ride the
Waves

Joe Friedman

Illustrated by Sam Childs

Orion
Children's Books

For Yvette,
You're one of
the first to
read the
latest book,
Joe Friedman

I'd like to thank Cliff McNish for help with the
Sabre Tooth Cave and my daughter Susie for help
with the Uncle Neill story. J.F.

First published in Great Britain in 2010
by Orion Children's Books
a division of the Orion Publishing Group Ltd
Orion House
5 Upper St Martin's Lane
London WC2H 9EA
An Hachette UK Company

1 3 5 7 9 8 6 4 2

Text copyright © Joe Friedman 2010
Illustrations copyright © Sam Childs 2010

A catalogue record for this book is available from
the British Library.

Printed in China

ISBN 978 1 84255 681 8

www.orionbooks.co.uk
www.boobela.com

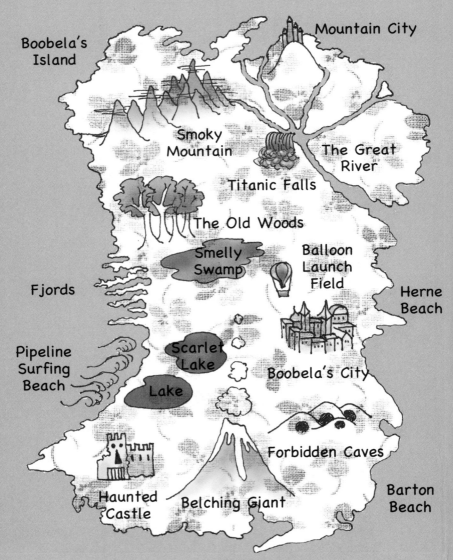

Gran's Island

Boobela's World

Mountain City

Boobela's Island

Smoky Mountain

The Great River

Titanic Falls

The Old Woods

Smelly Swamp

Balloon Launch Field

Fjords

Herne Beach

Scarlet Lake

Pipeline Surfing Beach

Lake

Boobela's City

Forbidden Caves

Haunted Castle

Belching Giant

Barton Beach

Contents

The Sabre Tooth Cave   9

Hide and Seek   43

Uncle Neill and the Magic Writing   71

Boobela and Worm Ride the Waves   99

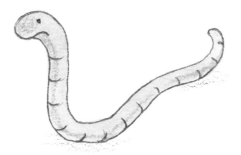

The Sabre Tooth Cave

Boobela hiked up the forest path. It was Worm's Name Day and he'd decided he wanted to see the Sabre Tooth Cave, the deepest of the Forbidden Caves. It was filled with stalagmites and stalactites that looked like sharp teeth.

Boobela hated the idea of being underground and having to squeeze through narrow, cold, slimy tunnels. But she'd agreed because Worm had done so much to help her.

They came out of the forest into bright sunlight. The entrance to the caves was ahead. Two boys were standing in front of it, looking at a map.

"I'm Andrew," the older boy declared in a loud voice. He stuck out his hand to shake Boobela's. "And this is my baby brother, Billy. We're going to the Sabre Tooth Cave."

Boobela introduced herself and Worm. "We're going there too! It's a treat for Worm."

"I want to see if stalagmites taste different from stalactites," Worm added. "Why don't we travel together?"

The boys agreed.

Andrew pulled two headbands out of his rucksack. They had lights attached so that he and Billy could see in the dark.

Boobela wished she'd thought of that! She'd just brought torches.

They entered the first cavern. It was airy and dappled with sunlight. This isn't so bad, thought Boobela.

But as they went into the tunnel at the end of the cave, they left the sun behind.

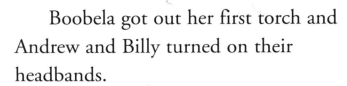

Boobela got out her first torch and
Andrew and Billy turned on their
headbands.

"I'll lead the way," Andrew declared.
He strode off down the passage.

Billy and Boobela followed. The
ceiling got lower and lower.
Boobela had to crouch to
walk. The tunnel ended
with a sudden drop.

Andrew jumped down first and Boobela slid off the ledge. She helped Billy down.

They found themselves in another small cavern. In the middle was a large rock covered with brightly-coloured crystals. The light from their torches was reflected by the crystals onto the ceiling.

"It's like a planetarium!" exclaimed Billy. "Isn't it wonderful?"

Boobela nodded. The dancing lights were magical.

Andrew wasn't interested. He just charged off down another low passage.

"Your brother likes to be out in front," Worm said to Billy.

"He always takes the lead," replied Billy sadly. "So I'll *never* be as brave or as heroic as him."

"You don't know that," Boobela protested.

"You can't know how brave you are until you're tested," Worm added.

Billy stared at the ground. *He* knew. He'd never be a hero.

* * *

The roof got so low
that soon they had to crawl.
The floor was slimy and cold.

"Be careful!" Andrew shouted from
up ahead.

Boobela and Billy slowed down. The
tunnel opened onto a narrow path along
the side of a sheer cliff face. The roof of
the cavern was high above them, the
ground far below.

Andrew had his back pressed up
against the cliff.

"Stay close," Andrew urged. "We
don't have to go very far." He beamed
his light ahead so they could see.

Billy followed Andrew, hugging the
wall and creeping sideways very slowly.

Boobela went last. She knew if she
slipped she'd never see her parents again.
She was very careful where she put her
large feet.

Andrew arrived at the end of path first. "I'm safe," he whispered.

Billy was next. "Me too."

Finally, the path widened and Boobela was on firm ground herself.

"That was scary," she said.

Even Andrew agreed.

The path headed downwards. At last, the three children were able to walk side by side.

19

"Listen," said Worm.

They stopped. They could hear the sound of running water. Soon they arrived at a raging torrent. On the other side was the Sabre Tooth Cave. They could see its large stalagmites and stalactites in the torchlight.

"They *do* look like teeth," Worm exclaimed.

"We need to find a way to cross," Boobela said.

"Here," shouted Billy. Four large smooth stones made a path across the water. They glistened in the torch light.

"They look slippery," Boobela worried.

"Don't fret," said Andrew. "I'll go last. That way I can save anyone who misses their footing."

Boobela glanced at Worm. She knew he was frightened of water.

"We've come all this way," he said. "I don't want to stop now."

"OK," she said. "I'll go first."

She
stretched her leg
to the first stone.
It felt solid enough.
She put her weight on
it, then stepped onto
the second stone. Her
foot slipped on a slimy
patch and she almost lost
her balance, but she
quickly corrected

herself and moved onto the third stone.

"That was close," breathed Worm. "The last thing I wanted was a cold bath on my Name Day."

One more step . . .

. . . and Boobela was over.

Billy followed, surefootedly hopping from stone to stone. Then Andrew confidently stepped onto the first stone. As he stretched to get to the second – disaster! He slipped on the same patch as Boobela but wasn't able to get his balance.

"Help!" he shouted.

It seemed to Boobela he was falling in slow motion. And that Billy had somehow speeded up.

Billy was running downstream along the rushing river. He seemed to be looking for something. Boobela ran after him.

When Billy came to the narrowest section of the torrent, he hesitated for a moment, then threw himself across, making a bridge that stretched from one side to the other.

Boobela immediately understood Billy's plan – his body would stop Andrew as the river swept him along. She bent down and grabbed his feet to steady him. In another moment, Andrew grabbed hold of Billy. Boobela held tight and, with a huge effort, pulled both boys onto the bank.

They all just lay there trying to catch their breath.

"You were brilliant," Worm said to Billy. "I told you that you never know how brave you are until you're tested."

"You're a proper hero," added Boobela.

Billy glowed.

Boobela looked to Andrew to add to the praise, but he seemed to be angry.

"I'm soaked," he muttered. Then he examined Billy. "*We're* soaked."

Boobela realized the two brothers were shivering uncontrollably.

"We don't have any dry clothes. We're already freezing," Andrew continued. "Even if we managed to struggle back, we'd be too ill to survive."

"I could get help," suggested Boobela.

"Think about it," Andrew replied grimly. "By the time any rescuers get here, it would be too late. My stupid mistake is going to kill us."

* * *

They lay in silence looking up at the stalactites. Then Boobela thought she saw a glimpse of light. But maybe it was just a reflection from their torches . . .

"Turn off your lights," she urged.

"Why?" asked Andrew.

"Just do what Boobela says," said Billy, feeling bolder because of his success in saving his brother.

The cave went completely black. It felt even colder without light.

"I see it!" shouted Billy. "There." He took Andrew's hand and aimed it towards a spot at the far right of the cavern. "Daylight!"

"You're right," Andrew agreed. Then, grudgingly, "Well spotted, Boobela."

"It could be another way out," suggested Worm.

They turned on their torches and
threaded their way between the huge
rock teeth rising from the floor of the
cave until they could see the light more
clearly.

"That's strange," said Boobela,
pointing at what looked a series of steps
along the side of the cave. They led to
the light.

"That's the Giants' Staircase," Billy said enthusiastically. "I read about it! But I never guessed that when I saw it I'd be *with* a giant!"

"I could climb out," Boobela realized. "Then, if I had a rope, I could pull you out."

Andrew pointed at his rucksack. "I have a rope – a very wet one. But I don't think you're strong enough to pull us out. It would take several giants to do that."

"If Boobela let down the rope, we could climb from step to step," Billy suggested.

Andrew sighed. "My hands and feet are already so numb I couldn't climb a ladder."

Boobela touched Andrew's hands. Then she held Billy's between hers. Billy hadn't been in the water but even his hands were as cold as ice cubes. They'd never be able to grip a rope. What were they going to do?

"Boobela?" Billy said tentatively after a few minutes.

Boobela was lost in thought. "What?"

"Something strange is happening. To your hands."

Boobela looked down. Her hands were glowing with heat. Her special magic!

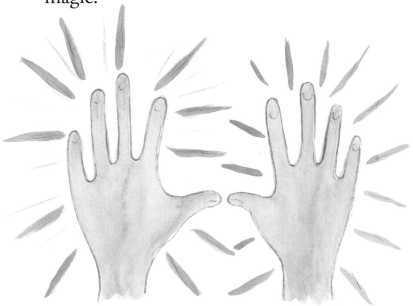

"I'm starting to feel things again," Billy whispered.

Boobela's hands continued to glow. She turned to Andrew. "Can you take off Billy's shoes?"

This time, Andrew didn't question Boobela's lead. He bent down and struggled to get Billy's shoes off with his numb fingers.

Boobela moved from Billy's hands to his feet. Then she held Andrew's hands.

"What's happening?" Andrew wanted to know.

"It's just a little something I can do at times. I call it special magic," Boobela replied.

Soon Boobela's magic work was finished. But Andrew and Billy's hands and feet wouldn't stay warm for ever. Now she had a climbing job to do.

* * *

Boobela took Andrew's rope and hung it around her neck.

"Ready?" she asked Worm.

"Slow and steady," he replied.

"Safety first," she agreed.

Then she
leaped upwards and
grabbed hold of the edge
of the first step. She pulled
herself up.

It was harder to pull herself on to the second step, though it wasn't quite as high.

I'm tired, Boobela thought.

She remembered the chocolate bar she'd put in her pocket before they started. It was still there, melted and squishy. But it tasted good, and restored her energy.

Boobela leaped for the third step. It was much higher and so it took three jumps before she could grab hold of it.

The fourth and fifth steps weren't so high but the sixth was really meant for a giant much bigger than her.

Finally, she was able to catch the edge and struggling, pulled herself up.

She stopped to catch her breath. Above her was a narrow passage leading out of the cave.

"I'm letting down the rope!" she shouted to Billy and Andrew. Her voice echoed through the stalagmites and stalactites.

She leaned over the edge of the step and fed the rope toward the ground.

"I've got it," Billy shouted.

Boobela left another couple of metres on the step where she was standing. This would trail after her up to the surface. Then she tied the remainder of the rope around her chest.

She examined the passage above her. It looked awfully narrow. The stairs were designed for giants, she thought, maybe this will be too.

Boobela clambered in. The passage sloped upwards and to the left.

She was able to crawl using her hands and knees at first, but the ceiling got lower and lower. Soon she had to wriggle on her belly. Then the sides got narrower and narrower.

Boobela felt scared. She was worried if she forced herself any further, she'd get stuck, unable to move either forward or backward. She froze.

"Keep looking at the light," Worm urged.

Boobela lifted her head until it bumped against the ceiling. Worm was right! It was easier to breathe when you were in daylight.

"Thanks, buddy," she whispered.

She inched forwards. The sides of the passage were so tight they pressed in on her ribs. But she kept her eyes on the light and forced herself further.

Finally, the passage began to open out. She gulped in air.

* * *

Soon she was standing in the sun. She stretched out towards the sky. It felt wonderful to have room to move again. But she had a job to finish. She tied the rope to a nearby tree, then returned to the hole she'd just left.

"I'm out and the rope's secure," she shouted.

She heard a faint echoey reply.

"We're on our way!"

It wasn't long before first Billy and then Andrew emerged from the hole.

"You saved our lives," Billy said, hugging Boobela's waist.

"And *you* saved my life," Andrew said to Billy. "You're both heroes."

Worm suddenly remembered something. "We were in such a rush to get out I didn't taste a stalagmite or a stalactite!"

Andrew took a piece of rock from his pocket. "This is from a stalagmite. I broke it off when I was resting on one of the steps."

"And this is from a stalactite," said Billy. "I found it while we were waiting for you to climb out."

Worm tasted both. Then he made a face. "They're both rubbish!"

"So you won't be wanting to go back to the Sabre Tooth Cave?" Boobela laughed.

"Not any time soon," agreed Worm.

"I can live with that," Boobela replied.

Hide and Seek

"I'm rubbish at games," Boobela complained.

"Enough!" Worm said, exasperated. Boobela had been going on about this for more than twenty minutes. "So, you're always the first to be found in hide and seek."

"I'm just too big."

"You're not *too* anything," Worm reminded her.

Worm understood. There were some things he was terrible at because he was so small, but that didn't keep him from *wanting* to be good at them.

"Why don't we go and see Gran?" he suggested.

"How can *she* help me be better at hide and seek?" sulked Boobela.

"I don't know," admitted Worm. "But she's never failed us yet."

* * *

Gran woke Boobela just after sunrise. She dressed quickly and installed Worm in his travelling box on her shoulder.

Gran led her to a path along the coast. They went up and down hills and along cliffs. Boobela struggled to keep up.

Finally, Gran stopped and pointed to a small hill at their side. She put her finger to her mouth.

Boobela climbed as silently as she could. She peeked over the top. There was a colony of rabbits sitting in the early morning sun about half a football pitch away.

What did Gran want her to do? Boobela looked back.

Gran gestured that she had to catch one. Boobela raised an eyebrow, but Gran shook her head. She wasn't going to explain.

Boobela crawled over the hill, feeling all heavy and awkward. The rabbit who was keeping watch saw her immediately. He thumped his foot on the ground. All the other rabbits stopped what they were doing and looked in her direction.

Boobela didn't know what to do. If she moved, the rabbits would bolt. Her stomach rumbled and she remembered she hadn't had breakfast.

She crept forward. **Thump, thump** went the lookout's foot. The rabbits disappeared into their burrows.

Boobela stood and returned to her Gran, who was sitting on a rock watching the waves.

"I didn't get near them," she confessed.

Gran nodded. Then she headed back along the path.

"Gran didn't expect me to catch a rabbit, did she?"

"Nope," agreed Worm. "I think this was a 'before.'"

"You mean, like when they have a photo of someone who is really thin and weedy and then an 'after' picture of them all strong and muscular?"

Worm nodded.

"What am I going to learn that makes me an 'after'?"

* * *

Granpa joined them for breakfast on Boobela's home-made veranda.

As they chatted, Boobela felt something rub against her leg. She looked down.

A small black and white kitten looked up at her and miaowed softly. Then he jumped onto Boobela's chest. His little claws went right through Boobela's rainbow T-shirt.

"Gently!" said Boobela.

The little cat understood. He pulled in his claws and settled down on her lap. Boobela stroked his back. The kitten purred.

"All animals have something to teach us," Gran said. "But you have to slow down and watch carefully."

Worm felt cross as he watched Boobela tickle the kitten. He regarded Gran suspiciously.

"And what is this *thing* going to teach Boobela?"

"When a cat hunts, he can be almost invisible. And that could be very useful to someone who wants to be better at hide and seek."

* * *

Boobela teased the kitten with a long stalk of grass. He batted at it. Then he tried to catch Boobela's hand.

"I'm going to call you Mischief," Boobela decided. She wondered if Worm would like the name. He'd been feeling out of sorts and so she'd let him stay with Gran.

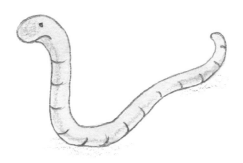

Mischief glanced at Gran's bird table. Two robins were eating seeds. Mischief moved a couple of steps, then froze.

Boobela watched, fascinated.

He crawled forward, then paused again. He was almost up to the table. The birds hadn't seen him approach. He wasn't invisible, but he was so still he might as well have been.

Mischief's weight shifted to his back legs. He was about to pounce.

Boobela clapped her hands. The robins flew off. Then she picked up Mischief, who was protesting, and carried him over a hill. She wanted privacy. So she could learn to move like her new friend.

* * *

When they were out of sight, Boobela threw a fabric dog bookmark into the tall grass. Mischief stalked it, creeping slowly, stopping, then pouncing.

Boobela realized that when Mischief was still even his thoughts stopped. When he jumped, his landing was light and precise.

She threw the dog bookmark again.

"This one's for me," she explained.

She took a crouching step, then tried to be quiet.

Soon, her legs ached and her thoughts rushed this way and that.

After a few moments, she couldn't bear it. She stretched her leg.

Mischief leaped alongside Boobela and then froze. He understood what she was doing!

Boobela knelt again. The pains came back and her thoughts started to wander.

Mischief put a little paw on her foot, as if to say, "Stop that!"

"It's hard," protested Boobela.

Mischief just stayed absolutely still, his attention on the bookmark.

Boobela relaxed and focused on the dog's head. To her surprise, her body stopped twitching and hurting so much.

Then Mischief crept forward.

Boobela moved her right leg as lightly as she could. The ground shook.

Mischief put his paw on Boobela. He was telling her to do it again!

Boobela moved eight times before Mischief was satisfied. The key to creeping quietly, she decided, was to think of herself as being as light as her balloon.

After each stalking game, Mischief leaped into Boobela's lap and she'd stroke him until he was purring like a little engine.

They played all afternoon. By the time the sun started to go down, Boobela was completely exhausted. She wondered how Worm was doing and if he was feeling better.

* * *

The following morning, Gran woke Boobela early again.

"The rabbits are waiting," Gran said. "Let's see how invisible you can be."

Boobela remembered yesterday's stalking lesson. She hoped Mischief had taught her enough to be an "after."

"I'll try . . ."

"Off you go then!" urged Gran.

Boobela picked up Worm's box and raised it to her eye. Worm was inside but he looked asleep.

Disappointed, Boobela put the box down. Worm's eye opened, just for a moment.

He's *pretending* to be asleep! Boobela thought. But why? Was something wrong? Of course not, she decided. He's just tired.

Boobela fastened Worm's case to her shoulder and set off down the coastal path.

* * *

After a while, Boobela noticed Mischief was following her, playing hunting games with the butterflies and grasshoppers along the way.

She stopped to watch and Mischief came up to her for a stroke. "Are you going to help me?"

Mischief put his paw on Boobela's foot.

Boobela laughed.

Worm poked his head out of his box. "Does that cat have to come *everywhere* with us?" Worm asked, annoyed.

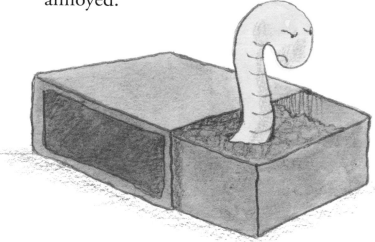

"I thought you were asleep."

It wasn't like Worm to be cross with her . . . Suddenly, she realized – he was *jealous*!

"You are and always will be my Number One buddy," she reassured him.

"I'm not furry . . ." worried Worm. He knew worms couldn't be petted like cats.

"No, but you're smart and loyal and everything I want in a friend."

Worm wasn't finished. "We're not taking him home with us?"

"Mischief belongs here," Boobela agreed. "On Gran's island."

And then Worm smiled for the first time since they'd met the little kitten.

* * *

Boobela decided to sneak up on the rabbits from the side. Mischief went with her. As soon as she came within sight, the rabbit lookout noticed.

Both Boobela and Mischief froze, staying completely still until the rabbit decided they were harmless and went back to eating.

Boobela took a light, crouching step forward. Mischief followed her. The rabbit stared. They stayed completely silent.

After a shorter time, he started grazing again. He hadn't thumped a warning signal!

Boobela and Mischief continued their slow progress, staying quiet for longer and longer as they got nearer the rabbits.

Finally, Boobela was close enough to pounce. She did. She reached for the closest rabbit but he was too fast for her and bounced away, uttering a warning cry. The rabbits disappeared.

"Very good!" Worm said.

That's what Gran thought, too. She gave Boobela a hug and Mischief some tuna. It was hard to tell who was happier.

"What have you learned?" Gran asked.

"Cats can't be invisible," Boobela said. "But they're so quiet, they're pretty close. I also discovered that if you really want to be still, you need to slow down your thoughts – even though it's hard."

* * *

The next day Boobela arranged to meet the Volcano Club in the gardens of the Town Hall. After a picnic lunch, the club decided to play hide and seek.

"I bet you'll be the first to be found," Joey said.

Boobela hoped that wasn't true. She looked around.

Should she hide
in the gazebo?

Behind the
statue of the
horse?

Or in the hedge near the lake?

She felt Mischief's presence. She
knew he'd say it didn't matter where she
hid, as long as she was still, but . . .

* * *

65

Boobela heard Rob shout, "Ninety-eight, ninety-nine . . ."

She dived behind a box hedge that had been cut into the shape of a teapot.

"Wouldn't over there be better?" worried Worm. "You may be quiet, but you're still big."

"Shussh," Boobela whispered.

She focused on her breathing. She'd discovered this was the best way to slow down her thoughts.

The noises around her faded.

A grasshopper started to climb up her leg, just as if she was a blade of grass.

It's working, she thought, excited.

Then she felt a tap on her shoulder. She turned to see Rob, Joey and two other members of the Volcano Club.

"I wasn't the first to be found!" Boobela enthused.

Rob looked puzzled. "I don't understand how I missed you the first time. Did you move?"

Boobela shook her head. Then she smiled mysteriously.

"I was as still as the grass."

* * *

The following morning, Boobela lay in bed, thinking about the dream she'd just had.

In the dream, Mischief had appeared and waved goodbye. Boobela knew they'd meet again. She remembered the dreams she'd had with Worm and that dreaming of an animal meant it was a true friend and guide.

Now she had two animal helpers, one distant and one close.

Letter from Mum and Dad

Boobela inspected the letter the postman had just given her. Her mum always used a red wax seal. It had been broken. And resealed. But not in the way her mum would have done it . . .

Worm was looking at the letter over her shoulder.

"Worm . . ." she began.

"Somebody has been interfering with your mail," he finished the thought.

Boobela opened the letter nervously.

There was only one page. Her mum hadn't drawn any of her usual funny pictures.

Dear Boobela,
We had really hoped to be on our way home now but every time we are about to leave, the medicine man we have been studying with suddenly "remembers" a new plant he has to show us. This means another delay of a few days. The last time the plant was not "new" and when we told him this he got very angry, and he had his warriors keep us in our hut for three days as a "punishment" for questioning him.

Your father and I are very worried that

Boobela turned the page – but there was no writing on the other side.

Worm knew what she was thinking.

"Somebody has removed the second page," he said.

Boobela had goosebumps. "Who would have done that?"

They looked at one another.

"The medicine man . . ." they said at exactly the same moment.

Worm knew that Boobela would be worried about her parents. "They'll figure out how to get away."

Boobela was reassured. But not totally. "I guess I can wait until their next letter . . ."

Uncle Neill
and the
Magic Writing

"I'm worried about Nurgul," Boobela said. "Even maths problems don't excite her any more."

"Why don't you ask her what's wrong?" asked Worm.

"I did! She said she was fine. I don't believe it."

The doorbell rang.

"Who could that be?" Boobela wondered.

She opened the front door. Her
Uncle Neill rushed in,
lifted her into the
air and spun her
in a circle.

Boobela squealed. *No one* lifted her any more. Except Uncle Neill.

"How's my favourite niece?" Uncle Neill exclaimed. He put her down and examined her more closely. "Worried," he answered his own question.

"One of our friends is very unhappy," Worm joined in.

"I'm sorry. I didn't say hello to you, little buddy."

"No hugging. No kissing. And *no spinning*," Worm said quickly. He was already feeling dizzy from being on Boobela's shoulder. Worm liked to move slowly and, if possible, in a straight line.

Neill laughed. "I hear you, Worm." He turned to Boobela. "What's bothering your friend?"

"We don't know," replied Boobela. "She *says* everything is fine."

"It sounds like we need some magic to find out what's really the matter," Neill concluded.

"Do you do magic?" asked Worm.

"Not magic like Boobela and Gran. I do stage magic."

And he pulled a red ball out of Boobela's nose.

Boobela laughed with delight. But she didn't want to get distracted. "Let's make a plan to find out what's wrong with Nurgul."

* * *

Uncle Neill, Boobela and Worm arrived at the Balloon Club just after noon. Everyone was sitting together eating their packed lunches. Everyone except Nurgul. She was sitting off on her own, reading a book.

"This is my Uncle Neill," Boobela said.

Uncle Neill, who was wearing his black magician's cloak and a big black hat, bowed deeply.

Boobela continued, "But he'd prefer to be called *Neill the Magnificent*."

Everyone laughed. Neill started his routine immediately. He walked up to Sophie and said, "You look like a girl who washes behind her ears." He peered behind her right ear. "But what's this?" He pulled out a lump of spaghetti. "Last night's dinner?"

Sophie giggled. "We had chicken last night."

"Maybe it was the night before," said Neill, moving on to Jacob.

"I can see this boy is a bird lover. Is that right?"

"I like looking at birds," Jacob admitted.

"I like birds too, but not—" Neill fiddled with Jacob's long hair "—in my hair!"

A parrot appeared. It squawked and flew over to Boobela.

Everyone roared with laughter and Jacob clapped. Nurgul couldn't help but be intrigued. She crept closer.

"Now, Neill the Magnificent will show he can read your most secret thoughts." Neill closed his eyes, spun in a circle, and pointed dramatically at Nurgul. "*You* need to have your mind read!"

"I don't really," protested Nurgul weakly.

"Go on," the other children urged. They wanted to see the trick. Boobela pushed Nurgul forward. Reluctantly she stood up.

Uncle Neill took a piece of paper from his cloak then, with a flourish, drew a shape in the middle.

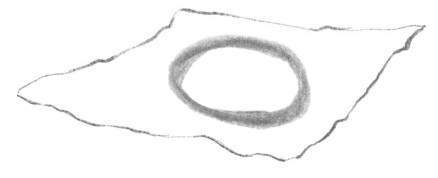

"This is the magic circle. You must write what you most want in the world inside it."

Neill turned away as Nurgul bent over and scribbled something in the circle.

"Scrunch it up," Neill said. Nurgul did. Neill took the balled-up paper and tore it into tiny pieces. Then he put the pieces on a little plate and set them on fire. "I forgot to ask – did you use joined-up writing?"

Nurgul shook her head. "I printed. Was that wrong?"

"Entirely my fault," Neill said, producing another piece of paper and drawing a circle in the middle. "This time, joined-up writing."

He twirled away. Nurgul scribbled, then scrunched up the paper. Neill turned, extended his hand and Nurgul tried to put the paper into it, but instead Neill reached into Nurgul's hood. He pulled out a pink envelope and handed it to her.

Still holding the balled-up paper, she opened it and read the sheet of paper inside. Her face turned white.

"How did you . . .!" Nurgul exclaimed.

Everyone applauded and cheered. Neill bowed.

Most of the children headed off to launch balloons for the afternoon flights. Boobela and Worm stayed behind with Uncle Neill.

"Why did you ask Nurgul to write in joined-up writing?" Worm wanted to know.

"Well spotted," Neill said. "That was the crucial moment. I needed something to distract everyone's attention to give me a chance to read what she'd written the first time, and prepare the pink envelope."

"What did she wish for?" Boobela asked.

"She wanted her parents to stop fighting."

"Why are they fighting?" Worm asked.

"We have to find out," Boobela declared. She thought for a moment. "I know! I'll invite her for a sleepover. It's easier to talk when it's late and the lights are out."

"And there won't be any problem with her parents because Uncle Neill is here. Brilliant!" said Worm.

* * *

Nurgul arrived just before dinner. She was carrying a little backpack which was mostly filled with a well-worn, large white stuffed toy dog.

"He's cute!" Boobela said.

"His name is Doggie."

"Hello, Doggie," said Boobela, tickling the dog's ear. "We're having a barbecue. Come outside."

Almost as soon as they sat down at the picnic table, Uncle Neill put the food on the grill: corn on the cob, hamburgers and hot dogs.

Boobela sniffed deeply. "It smells wonderful."

Nurgul nodded.

They ate until they were stuffed.

"Now," Uncle Neill declared, "it's time for some more."

"I couldn't eat another thing," Boobela said, sighing.

"You don't understand," Uncle Neill laughed. "Everyone can eat *s'mores*."

"What's a s'more?" Nurgul wanted to know.

"Watch!" Uncle Neill toasted some marshmallows on the barbecue, then made a sandwich with digestive biscuits on the outside and marshmallow and chocolate inside.

"I love chocolate!" Nurgul said enthusiastically. She was definitely feeling better.

Neill put the s'mores on the grill and when the chocolate and marshmallows had melted together he put them on the table. "You don't have to eat them if you don't want to . . ."

Everyone had three helpings.

By then, it was time for bed. The girls went up to Boobela's room. Worm stayed with Uncle Neill.

"I hope this works," Worm said. "I don't like it when someone's unhappy."

"Neither do I, little buddy," agreed Neill.

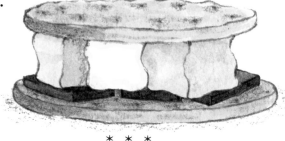

* * *

"I don't need a pillow," Nurgul said. "I always sleep on Doggie."

She lay down on the mattress Boobela had prepared next to her bed. Boobela turned out the lights.

At first, they talked about what was happening at the Balloon Club. Then Boobela told Nurgul how she worried about her parents, because they were so far away from help if anything happened to them.

Nurgul spoke softly. "I . . . have a friend whose parents are arguing a lot."

"Do you know why they're arguing?"
Boobela asked.

Nurgul paused. "They had a fight.
Not a big one. But after it, they found
that a statue of the two of them had
been broken. It was a wedding present.
Each of them thought the other had
done it."

"What *really* happened?"

". . . my friend broke it. By mistake. She was too ashamed to tell her parents and now she's worried they will keep arguing until they break up."

Boobela knew that Nurgul was talking about herself. "If I were you, I'd encourage your friend to confess to her parents."

There was a long silence while Nurgul thought about what Boobela said. Then she seemed to make a decision. "Maybe you're right."

* * *

The next morning at breakfast, Nurgul told them how she'd broken her parents' statue.

"I thought it was your friend," Boobela protested, acting as if she was surprised.

Nurgul smiled. She was pleased she'd fooled Boobela.

"I've decided to make them a replacement," she went on. "The thing is . . . the first statue was really beautiful and I'm not very good at making things . . ."

"I wouldn't worry about that," said Uncle Neill. "I've loved everything Boobela made for me."

"Really?" Nurgul asked.

"Especially when she put her heart into it."

"I'll make the statue with all my heart," Nurgul said firmly.

91

She set to work immediately. Worm helped her choose the best clay from the garden. Neill and Boobela helped make the base, and Nurgul struggled for several hours to get a good likeness of her parents. Finally, she was finished.

"It's beautiful!" Boobela exclaimed. "Let's go and show your mum and dad." The two of them set out.

Worm decided to stay with Uncle Neill who was going to clean the barbecue. He wanted to taste the ash.

* * *

Nurgul's house was just ahead. Her parents were sitting on the porch.

Boobela handed Nurgul the parcel with the sculpture in it. "Good luck!" she said.

"Come with me," Nurgul pleaded. "I'm not sure I'll be able to do this on my own."

Boobela agreed. They went up to the house together.

"How was the sleepover?" Nurgul's mum asked.

"It was great," Nurgul said. Then she said softly, "Mum, Dad, I have something to tell you."

Boobela stood beside Nurgul and put a supportive hand on her back.

Nurgul took a deep breath. The words tumbled out. "I broke the wedding statue. I'm really sorry. And I'm sorry I didn't admit it right away. I was ashamed. I made you another one. It's not the same but it was done with all my heart."

Her parents looked at one another. Her father took her mum's hand. Nurgul handed her parents the package. They unwrapped it and just looked at it a long time.

Nurgul started to get nervous. She thought they didn't like it.

"It's lovely," her mum said.

"Beautiful," breathed her dad. "It's better than the original."

"I'm sorry I made you argue so much," Nurgul said.

"That wasn't your fault," her dad replied. "I should have believed your mum."

"And I should have believed your dad," her mum agreed.

Nurgul rushed up to her parents and they all hugged each other. Boobela felt like crying herself. She was glad it had turned out well for Nurgul but . . . she wished she could hug *her* parents.

* * *

Back at the house, Boobela told Uncle Neill and Worm what had happened.

Worm remembered his big argument with Boobela. "I'm glad you helped them sort things out. It's horrible to argue with someone you care about."

Boobela knew what Worm meant. "Absolutely."

"Nurgul is lucky to have such good friends," Uncle Neill said, looking at Boobela and Worm fondly. "How are we going to celebrate?"

Boobela and Worm looked at one another.

"More magic tricks!" they both said at exactly the same time.

Uncle Neill laughed. "I'm not much of a mind-reader! I should have guessed!"

He went over to his backpack and started preparing a very special show.

Boobela
and Worm
Ride the Waves

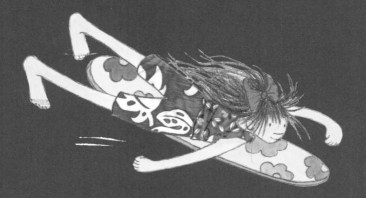

As Boobela folded her balloon, she
looked around at Pipeline Beach.

On the sand, people were waxing
their surfboards and having lessons.

The water was full of boys and girls
paddling out to where the surf was
breaking, waiting their turn to catch a
whitecap, or riding the waves.

There was so much going on, she
hardly knew where to look.

An older, blond boy came up to Boobela. "Need any help?" he asked.

Boobela shook her head. "I will later, when I launch. I'm Boobela. This is my pal, Worm."

"I'm Mark." He looked at Worm. "You're quite a dude, aren't you?"

Worm smiled. "Call me Daddy Cool."

"OK, Mr Cool," said Mark, laughing. He turned to Boobela. "Here for the surfing?"

Boobela pointed to a dark-haired girl who was riding backwards and forwards along a large wave. "I want to surf like her."

"That's Raven," said Mark. "She won the championship. It'll take a while before you're as good as she is."

"Then I'd better get started," said Boobela. "Do you know anyone who could give me a lesson?"

Mark grinned. "I might."

He led her down to the water. People stopped to watch Boobela, but she was used to that now.

Raven got off her board and Mark gave her a kiss. Boobela realized Raven was his girlfriend!

"I'd like you to meet Boobela and Worm," he said.

Raven smiled. "Pleased to meet you," she said. "You *are* a big girl."

Boobela smiled shyly. She'd never met a champion before.

"Boobela wants to surf," said Mark. "Do you think you can get her up in a day?"

Raven playfully hit Mark on the shoulder. "You know I never turn down a challenge."

* * *

Raven took Boobela over to a strange-looking machine. A couple of old surfboards had been fixed onto rollers and wooden planks.

"Try standing on this," said Raven. "It's the closest thing to surfing,"

Boobela stepped on. The boards kept shifting under her feet.

She almost fell. But in time, she stepped off.

Raven explained. "You need to keep trying."

Boobela jumped on the board and was pitched off.

"Use your arms to balance – it helps at the beginning," Raven suggested.

Two boys arrived. One was an older, dark-haired teenager, with a sour face. The other was Boobela's age.

"Hi, Richard," Raven said to the teenager.

Richard didn't answer. He looked Boobela up and down and laughed. "Clumsy, isn't she?"

"Her *name* is Boobela. We all were clumsy when we started," replied Raven mildly.

"I bet Sandy won't be as awkward as . . . *her*."

No one had been this rude about Boobela in ages. She didn't know what to say.

Worm did. "Did his mum forget to teach him manners?" he asked Raven.

Raven laughed. "Richard is angry because I beat him in the competition last week."

"You were lucky," Richard growled.

"You'll get another chance next year." Raven shrugged.

"Next thing he'll be challenging me to a fight," said Worm, drawing himself up to his full height.

Boobela and Mark giggled at the thought.

Richard frowned. "I'm a much better teacher than you. Sandy will be surfing way before your *friend*," Richard replied.

He stalked off. Sandy followed, reluctantly.

"He's horrible!" exclaimed Worm.

Raven nodded. "Some boys hate to be beaten by girls." She turned to Boobela.

"Ignore him," Raven continued. "You can't let him spoil this beautiful beach."

Boobela nodded. She was hurt and she didn't feel able to speak.

Seeing this, Worm said, "You came here to learn to surf. You've got a great teacher. The sky is blue and the sun is warm. Are you going to let Richard spoil your day?"

Worm was right! Boobela got back on the surf simulator. She lasted almost a minute.

"Great!" said Raven. "A couple more tries and I'll teach you to pop up."

"What's popping up?" asked Boobela.

"It's when you stand on your board just before you ride a wave."

"Does everything in surfing have a special name?"

"Almost," said Raven, laughing.

* * *

As Boobela practised, Raven went to look for a board. When she returned, she was carrying one that was much bigger than her.

Boobela took the board in her hands. "It's hard to believe I could stand on this in the water."

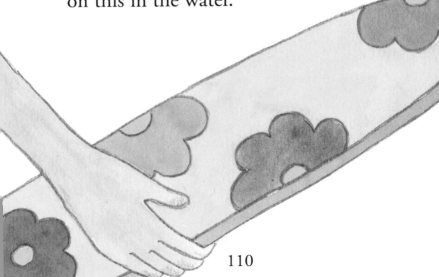

Raven smiled. "Maybe not *quite* yet. But you *can* learn to paddle."

On the beach, Boobela saw Richard glaring at her as Sandy did pop-ups in front of him. Raven followed Boobela's eyes, then gave Boobela a sympathetic look.

"I know," said Boobela, sighing. "I can't let him ruin this beautiful beach. Why does he dislike me so much?"

Raven shrugged. "It's nothing to do with you. And I don't think Sandy likes it either."

"Don't worry, pardner," said Worm. "I'll keep an eye on that mean varmint."

Boobela laughed. "I feel safer already. But if I'm going in the water, you'll have to keep watch from the land."

* * *

"Mark!" called Raven.

Mark came over. Boobela took Worm's travelling box and attached it to his shoulder.

Worm looked around. "Everything looks different at this height!" he exclaimed.

Mark laughed. "We're going to have a great time, dude."

Boobela and Raven walked out into the water until it was up to Boobela's waist. Raven had to stay in shallower water. She was up to her shoulders.

"Try lying on it," she said. "Don't be worried if you fall off."

Boobela lunged onto the board. It immediately rolled over and she came up coughing and spluttering.

"Now try getting on slowly."

Boobela wriggled on. Then she tried
to move her arms. The board went end
over end, soaking her again.

113

"Too far forward," Raven said.

Boobela tried again. This time she was too far back. She crept forward. She started paddling. The board stayed under her.

"Great," said Raven.

"This is fun!" Boobela replied.

* * *

Raven and Boobela joined Mark and Worm for lunch. They sat on a towel and ate sandwiches. Worm didn't fancy sand.

He ate some loam Boobela had brought along.

After lunch, Mark and Raven held hands and told surfing stories.

Boobela tried to listen. But she kept imagining Richard staring at her. She felt embarrassed that she couldn't follow Raven's advice and ignore him.

Worm noticed that Boobela's forehead was furrowed. "Is it Richard?" he asked.

Boobela nodded.

"He's a bully," Worm said. "Did you know you're taller than him?"

"Really?" As Worm had guessed, in Boobela's mind Richard was much bigger than she was. Boobela realized that was because she was scared of him. Her gran had taught her what to do when she was frightened.

Boobela closed her eyes and went to the Fear Tree. After she'd hung her fear on its branches, she felt much better.

"Time to practise pop-ups," said Raven. "This time on the simulator."

Boobela tried several times before she could keep her balance.

"You're really improving," encouraged Worm.

Just then, Richard strode up to them, with Sandy trailing in his wake.

"Ready to wipe out big time?" he asked Boobela sarcastically.

Now, Richard looked just like an ordinary boy. And Boobela knew just what to say.

"Do you pick on everyone or just tall girls?"

Richard was taken aback. "Have you been getting bravery lessons?"

"How brave do I have to be to stand up to a bully like you?"

Richard blinked. "Come on, Sandy," he said, but he didn't sound so confident now.

"I'd prefer to stay," Sandy replied.

Richard stormed off, alone.

"That was very impressive," Raven said to Boobela.

Boobela blushed. "Can we take Sandy out with us?" she asked.

"Of course," said Raven.

* * *

There was a queue of surfers where the waves were breaking. Raven explained what they needed to do.

Boobela felt excited and a bit scared. "Do you want to go first?" she asked Sandy.

Sandy shook his head. "You earned it," he replied.

"Don't worry if you don't make it the first time," said Raven. She sat up on her board so she could watch Boobela and Sandy. "Ready?"

Boobela nodded. "That one's yours! Go!"

Boobela turned her board sideways and paddled as hard as she could into the wave.

The wave started to break. She popped up and tried to stand but the board was rocking and shifting in the white water.

She battled to keep her balance · · ·

Then she started to fall.

Just before she went under, Boobela inhaled swiftly. The next moment, she was being tumbled round and round by the wave above her. She held her breath.

After what seemed like minutes, the swirling water calmed down and Boobela was able to push her way to the surface.

A moment later, she saw Sandy's head emerge. He struggled to breathe. Boobela swam over to him.

"I wiped out too," Sandy exclaimed between breaths.

"It's like being in a washing machine under there," Boobela gasped.

Sandy pointed. "There are our boards."

They swam towards them, then, back into the shore.

Mark met them in the water at the waters edge. "Are you OK?" he asked.

Boobela and Sandy nodded.

Boobela imagined Worm tumbling in the water. "I'm glad you weren't with me," she said. She turned to Sandy. "We have time to catch one more wave. What do you think?"

"Absolutely," Sandy replied.

* * *

Raven joined them in the queue for waves.

"That was good for a first attempt," she encouraged. "Boobela, you started to stand a bit too late – do it before the wave breaks."

"There's so much to remember, all at the same time!" Boobela complained.

"That's what it's like learning something new," Raven agreed.

Boobela's turn arrived swiftly.

"Go!" Raven urged.

Boobela got her board into position. The water started to foam around her feet.

Now or never, she thought.

She popped up. The white water reached her knees. The wave continued to break. Boobela leaned forward. The wave pushed her faster and faster.

She was surfing!

Suddenly, the wave slowed and Boobela lost her balance. She held her breath as the wave crashed over her.

She came up, caught her board, and turned to watch Sandy. He managed to ride for a few moments before he fell in.

He came up near Boobela, spluttering and laughing. "That was great," he shouted.

They watched as Raven caught a wave and surfed all the way to the shore. They paddled in to join her.

Mark and Worm were waiting for them.

"You both did really well," Worm enthused.

Boobela said to Raven, "You're a champion teacher." She bent down and gave Raven a hug.

Worm looked at the setting sun. "We've got to rush," he said.

"Why don't you stay with us tonight?" asked Mark. "You could ride more waves tomorrow."

Boobela looked at Worm. He nodded. "We'd love to," she replied.

That evening on the beach, there was a barbecue and party that lasted until late. Boobela missed most of it, though. She was curled up on a blanket, fast asleep, a very tired giant.